caught in the rain

by beatriz ferro

illustrated by michele sambin

Where can you go when you are caught in the rain? For a small person, the possibilities are endless—under a broad mushroom, or Daddy's overcoat, beneath a floppy hat, or even an overturned rowboat. As each page is turned, children will delight to discover an imaginative new hiding place depicted in soft watercolor drawings.

CAUGHT IN THE RAIN gently captures the mood of a warm, rainy day. It is a perfect lap book for parent and very young child to enjoy reading together.

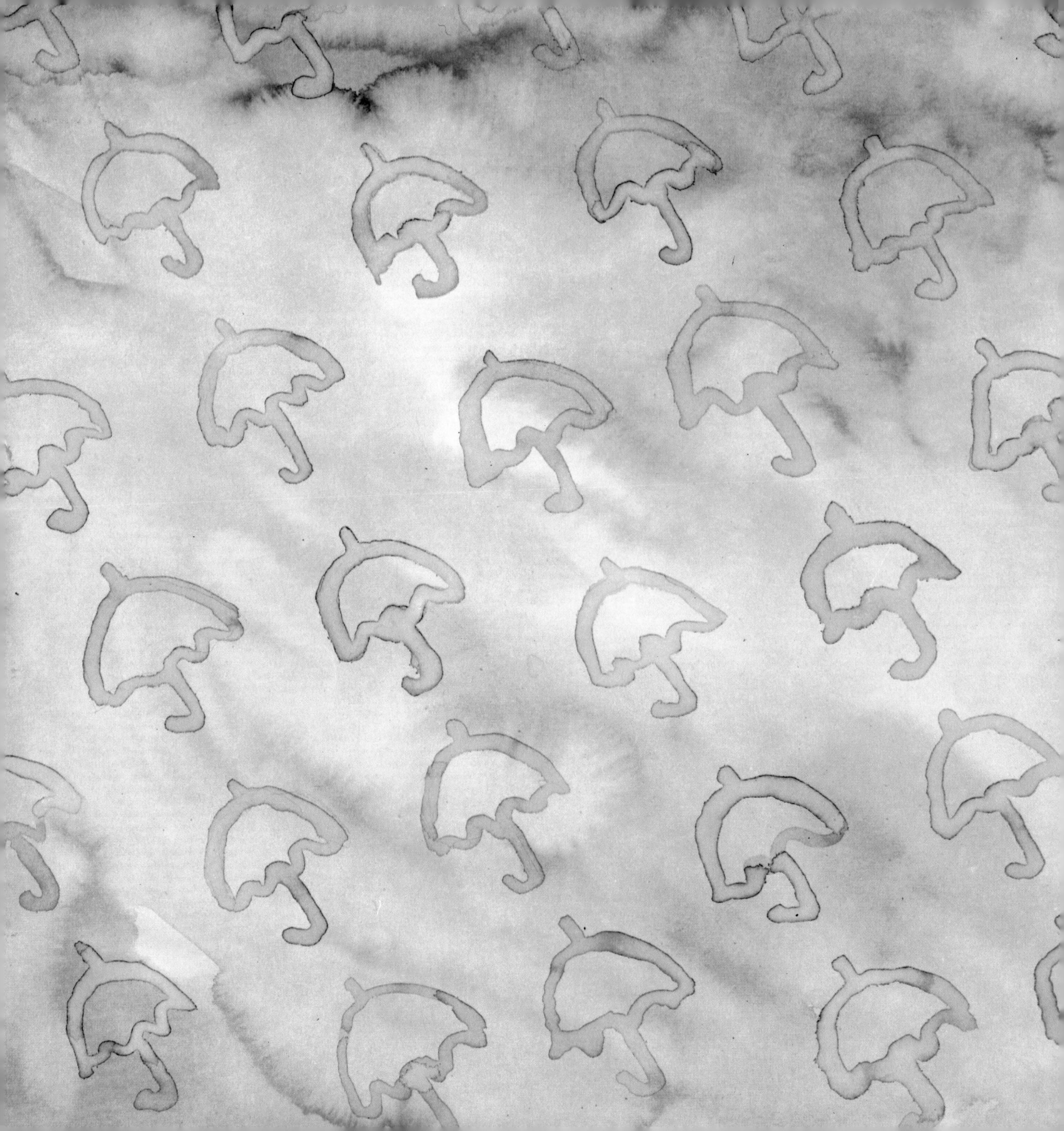

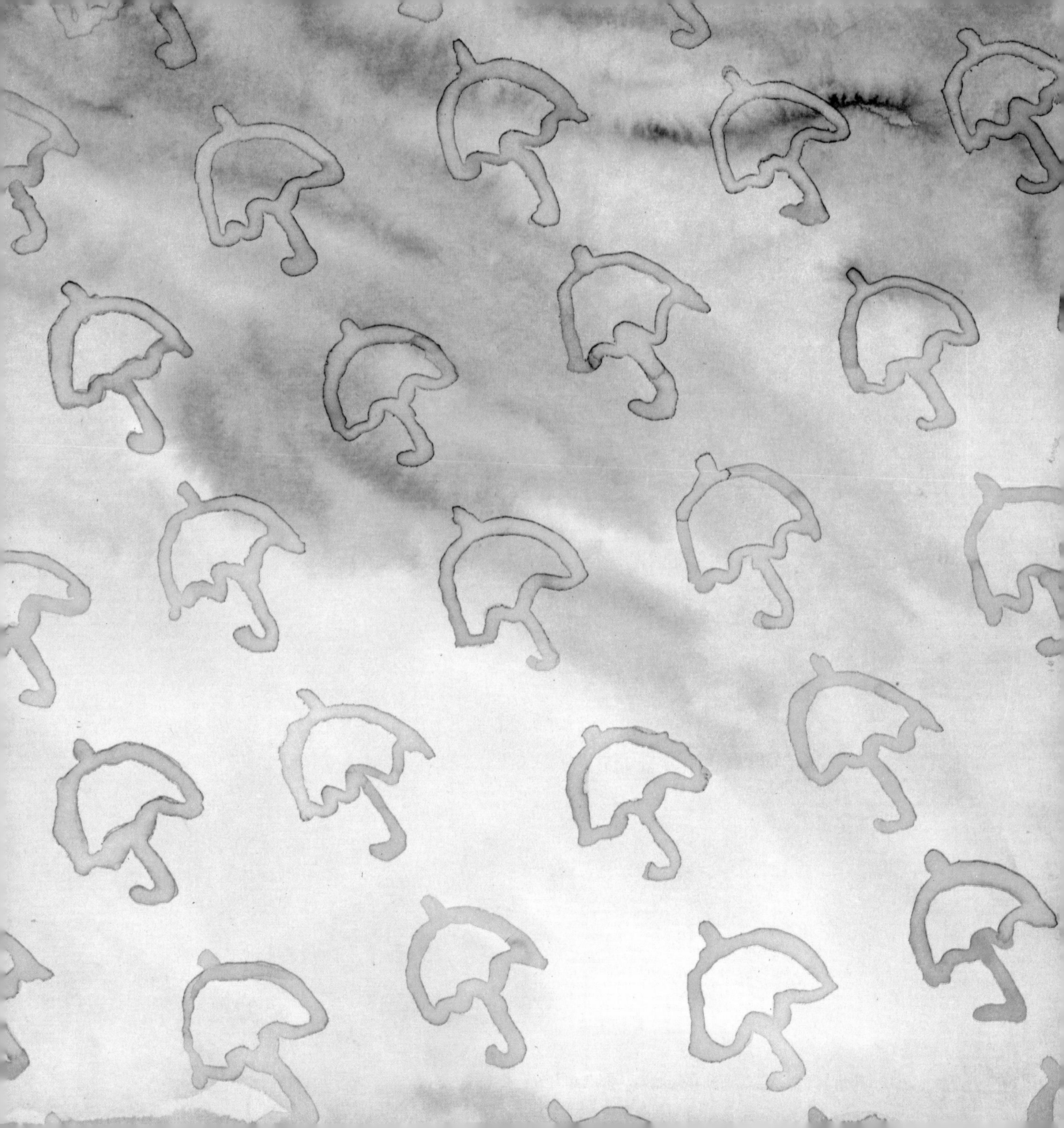

caught in the rain

by beatriz ferro

illustrated by michele sambin

Library of Congress Catalog Card Number 79-2513. ISBN 0-385-15624-3 trade. ISBN 0-385-15625-1 prebound. First Edition in the United States of America. Printed in Italy. First published in Italy, 1978, as *Per Esempio un Ombrello*, by Emme Edizioni.

When you are caught out in the rain a tree can keep you dry,

and so can a broad mushroom, if you are very small.

A wagon can keep you dry,

and so can a floppy hat.

A bridge will hide you from the rain
if you go underneath it.

The grocery awning blocks the rain,

and so does the morning paper.

Birds stay dry in a hole
in the wall,

or beneath a friendly statue.

You can be dry on a downtown bus,

or under Daddy's overcoat.

Even a boat upside-down on the beach will keep the rain away.

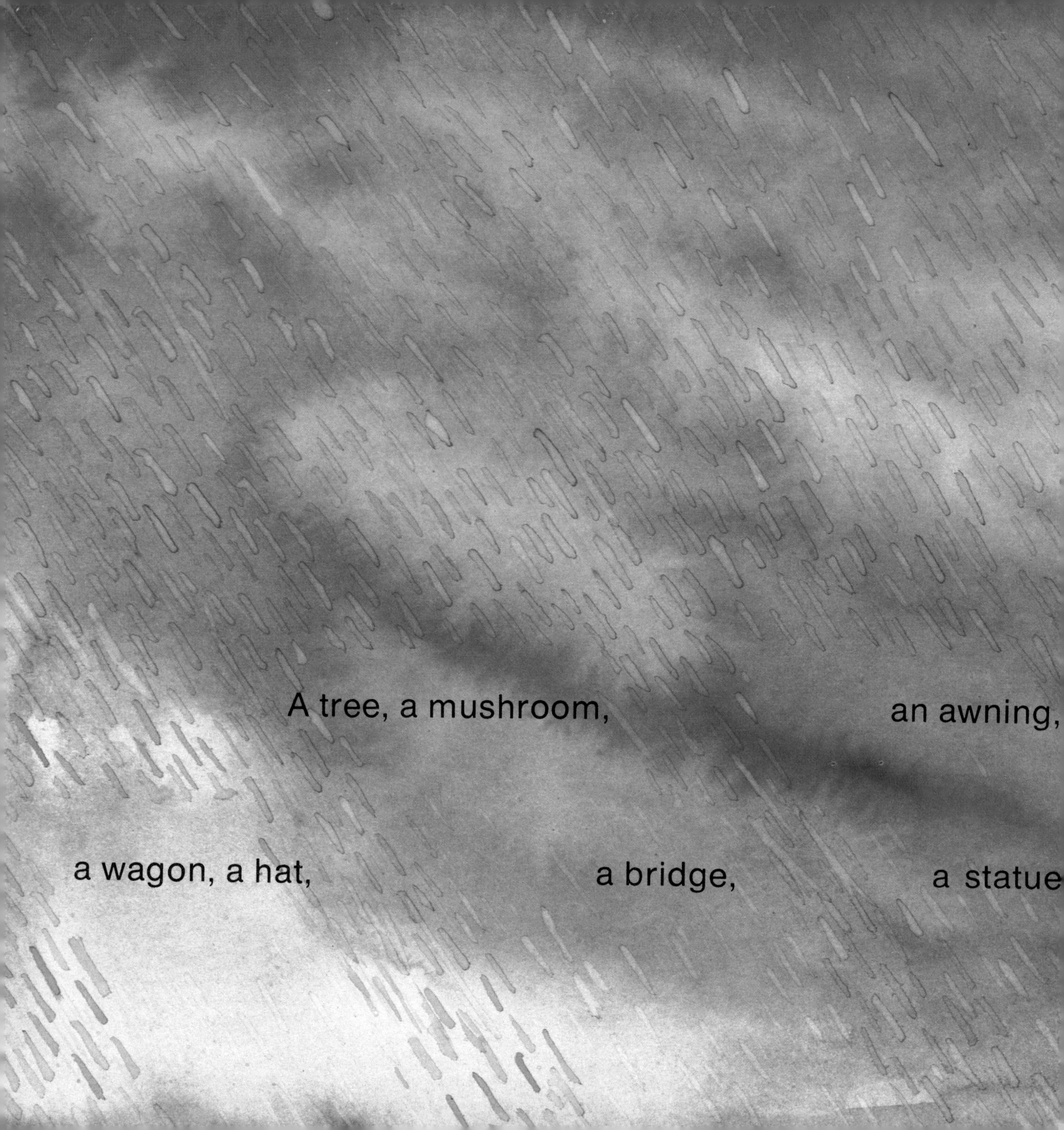

A tree, a mushroom, an awning,

a wagon, a hat, a bridge, a statue

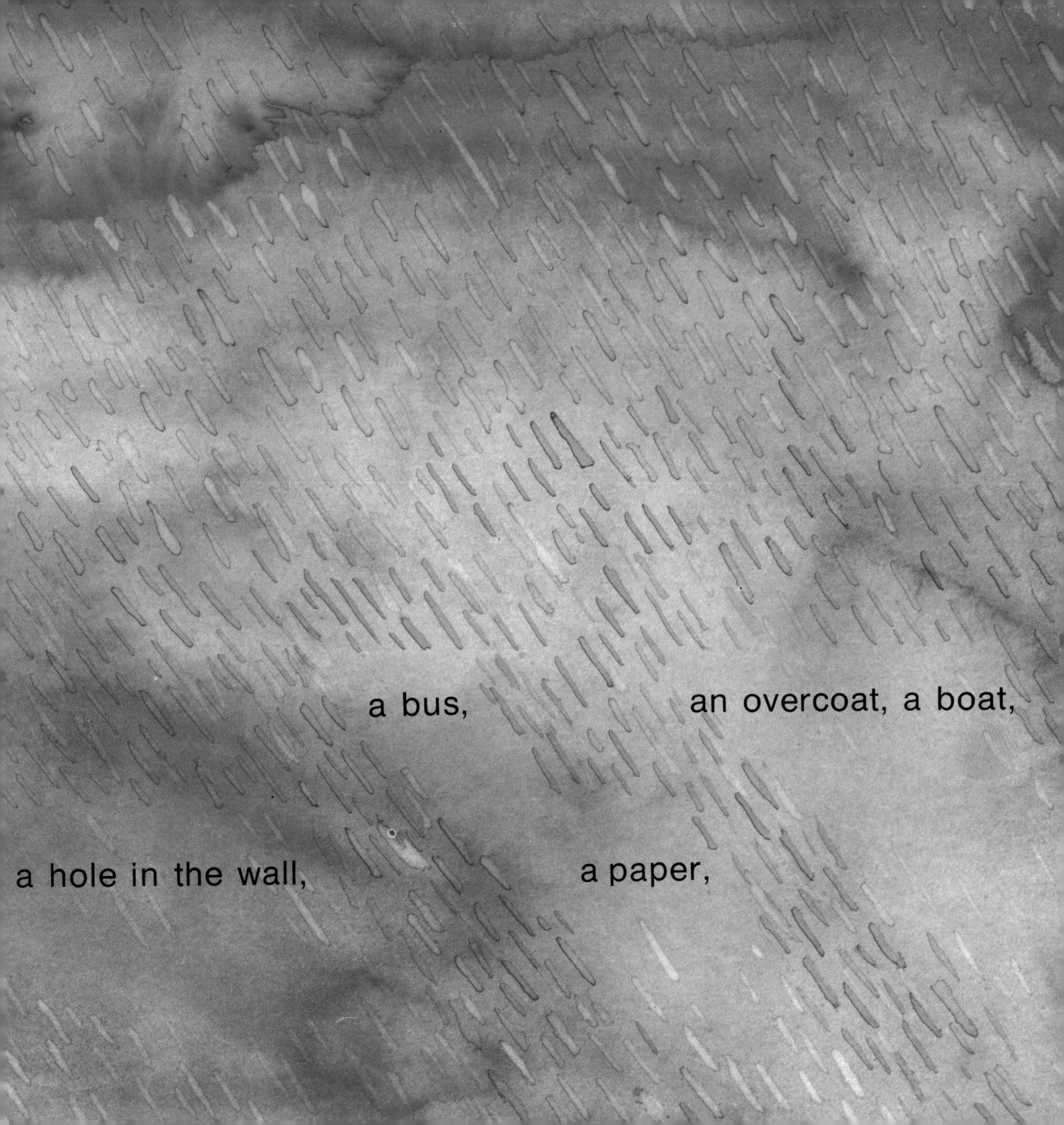

a bus,

an overcoat, a boat,

a hole in the wall,

a paper,

each of these is like a roof
that keeps you under cover.

But the very best way to get out of the rain
is by using an umbrella!

t's a portable roof you can hold in your hand.

You can carry it anywhere.

It will keep you dry wherever you are

when you get caught in the rain.

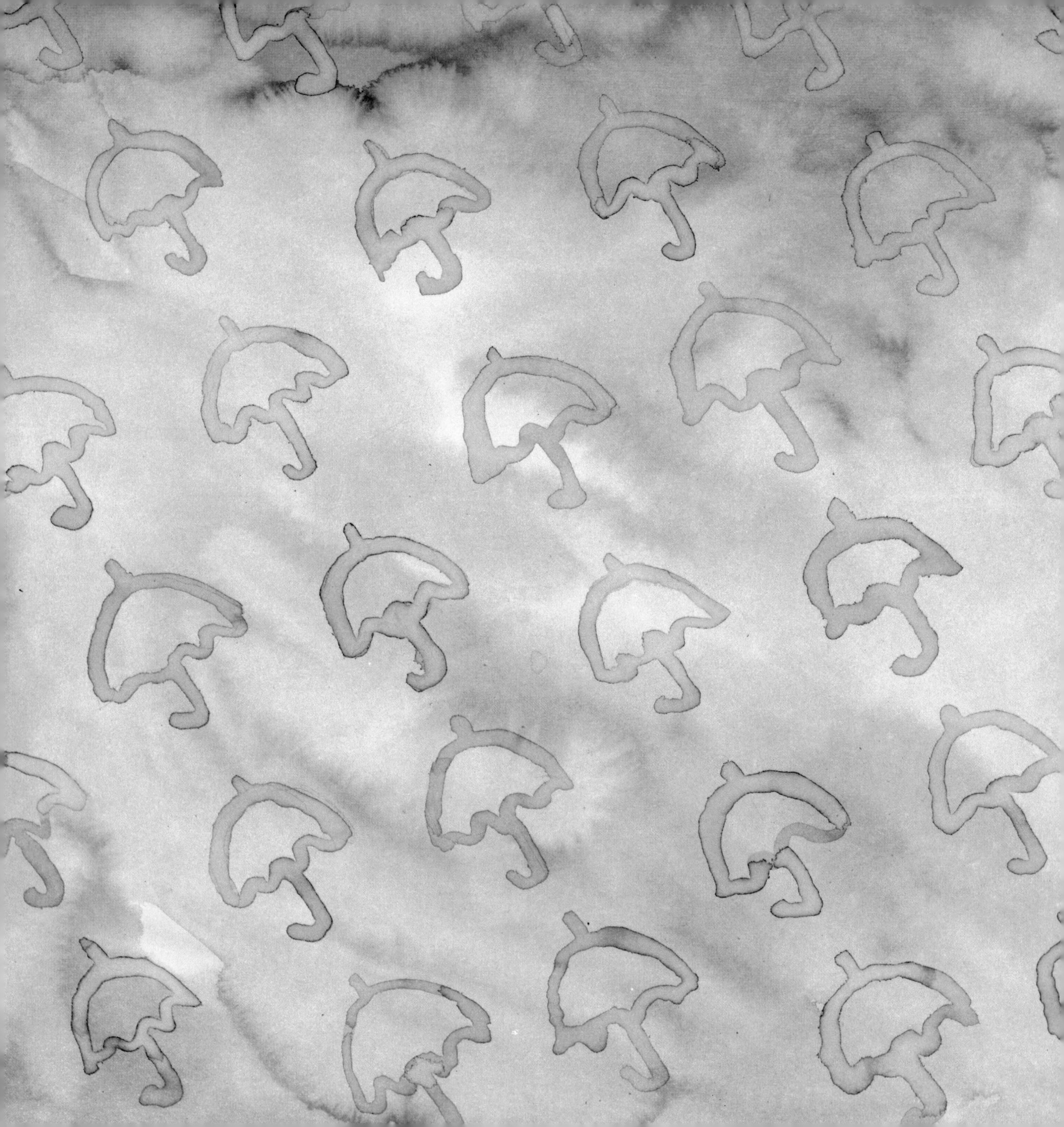

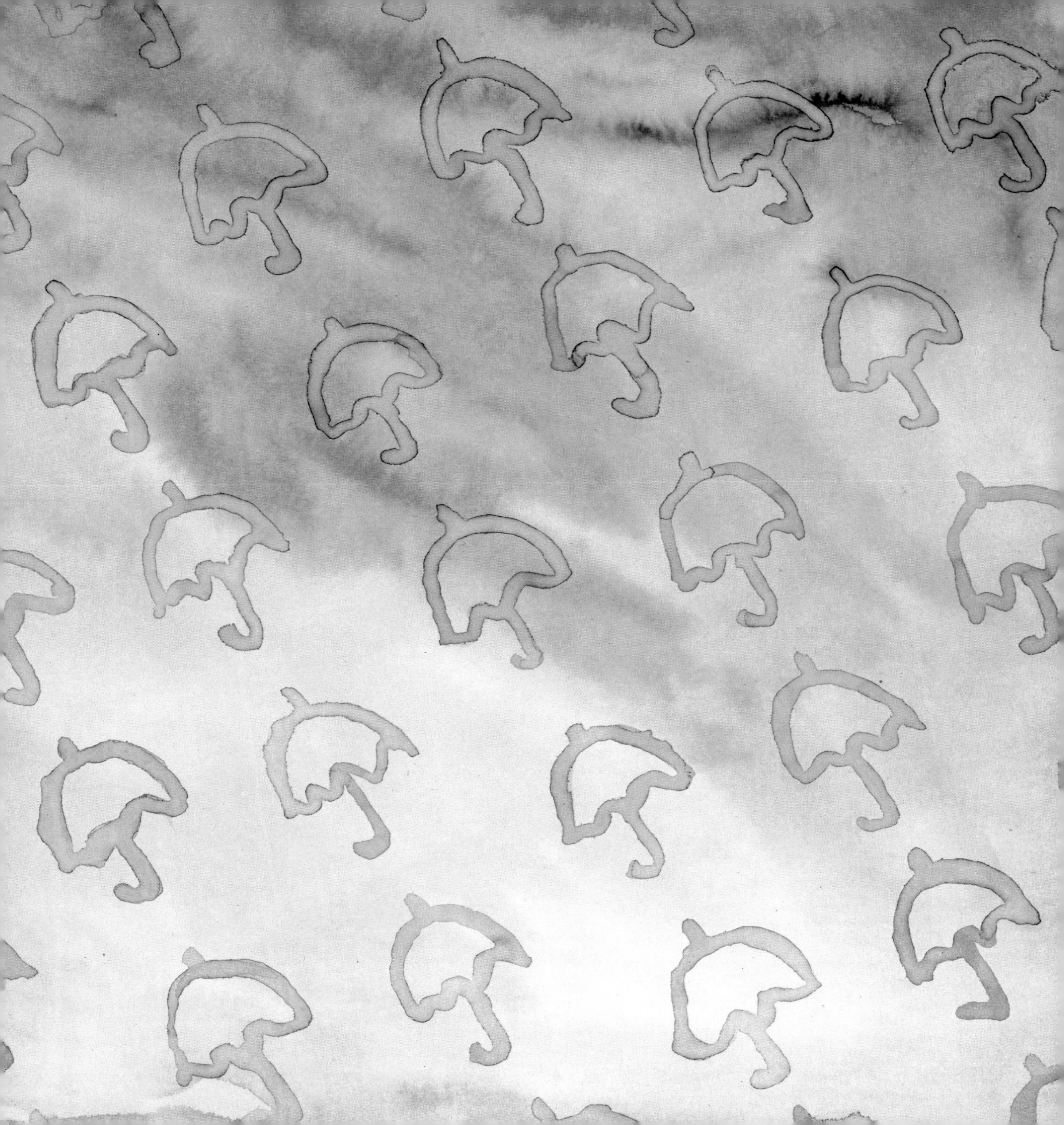